HARVEST

A Short Story from the Pumpkin Patch

Jason H. Abbott

This is a work of fiction. Names, characters, places, and incidents are either the product of the author's imagination or are used fictitiously. Any resemblance to actual persons, living or dead, events, or locales is entirely coincidental.

For more information, address:
Blue Boar Press
PO Box 204
Springvale, Maine 04083

Cover
Kate Whitmore

ISBN: 978-1-951478-02-5 (paperback)
ISBN: 978-1-951478-03-2 (ebook)

www.JasonHAbbott.com
www.BlueBoarPress.com

For Ray Bradbury,
who brought me to the Halloween Tree.
I've never left it.

Edgar awoke lying on cool dirt and with the taste of pumpkin seeds in his mouth. He rolled off his back in total darkness, a groggy lurch for a handhold only finding the rustle of an autumn leaf pile against his bare body.

Fumbling and blind, he rose and tried to spit the seeds out. But his lips were bound shut.

No.

His lips were *missing*.

With a muted grunt of panic, he attempted to press tongue against teeth and force his mouth open. Yet as fingers reached his face, he found he lacked a tongue in the same way he now lacked lips. Or teeth. Or a mouth of any sort to speak of... or with.

Instead his hands found a surface slightly ribbed and smooth. He could feel his fingers slide across it as if it were the skin of his face, but the texture was hard, hairless and utterly unlike the head he'd previously owned. He found it devoid of any features. Bubbling somewhere deep within him, the horrific realization that he wasn't in the dark but instead lacking any eyes at all announced itself with a muffled scream.

He stood groping whatever oblong and squat excuse for a head he now possessed. Clawing fingers grasped neither ears nor nose, or even hair. But when his farmer's grip touched the thick, curled stem atop his head, he recognized it for what it was at last.

"*Mumf-kin!*" came a muted cry from somewhere within the pumpkin-headed man's gourd.

In a panic, Edgar ran in whatever direction he was facing as he screamed something indecipherably muffled through inches of pumpkin flesh. His headlong sprint brought a rush of cool air that hinted he was naked, and the waist-high fencepost crashing into his crotch a moment later confirmed it.

He slid off the post, flopping to the ground with a garbled moan.

Edgar curled up, cringing in pain. Then the long bay of a dog was heard. Lifting his pumpkin head, he rubbed the sore spot the fall had left on the back of his gourd. The barks grew louder, and moments later paws skidded to a halt in the dirt and leaves beside him. A growl and snap of jaws greeted him as he rolled to confront the unseen animal.

"What the devil's goin' on? Who's out there?"

Hearing the woman's voice, Edgar raised himself up on an arm and frantically waved for help while fending off the nipping hound.

"If you're lookin' to steal somethin', ya'll ain't gonna find nothin' 'sides my dog's teeth in your ass!"

Edgar heard the crunch of footsteps approach on the autumn ground. In response, he sat up, raised arms in surrender, and mumbled out a plea that begged far more in tone than words.

The footsteps stopped, and there was the dull clank of a tin lantern hitting the ground. "Oh my stars an' the moon above!"

He shoved one hand higher and pointed to his pumpkin head with the other. "*Melp!*"

There was the crinkle of leaves crushed under a skirt when she kneeled beside him. "You poor thing! That bad old witch got you, didn't she?"

The mention of the witch provoked a vigorous nod from Edgar as the hound began barking anew.

"Now you hush-up, Squash-Dog!" she scolded, quieting the animal before it whined in complaint. "An' be nice!"

He felt her long fingers grip his shoulder, and she tugged him into sitting straight. "Can you understand me?"

The gourd nodded.

"Oh Sugar, that's good, 'cause I know you're mighty scared right now. But can you trust me and hold still for a minute?"

Edgar nodded again, hearing something pulled from her belt.

"Alright then. Now, I'm gonna make it a lot better... but I also ain't gonna lie. This'll sting a bit first."

She touched a knife's flat edge to Edgar's pumpkin cheek, and he flinched away from the cold steel.

"You need a *face*," she said, "an' I'm gonna carve you one."

His trembling palm rose, touching her hand and staying the first thrust of the blade.

"Now Sugar, do you wanna' stumble around blind and mute? Or do you want eyes for seein' and mouth for eatin' and conversin'?"

Edgar's hand lost its tremble, and after a slow pumpkin nod he lowered his fingers.

"Alright. And don't you worry, I'm really good at this!"

He squeaked as she made the first knife thrust into his gourd unannounced. She pulled out the blade, then made her second stab.

"I'm givin' you eyes first, 'cause everythin's less scary if you can see."

Edgar winced as the knife withdrew a second time, then plunged in again. The new slice connected the two prior cuts into a triangle.

"I reckon it's worse than a haircut, but ain't *quite* as bad as cuttin' your fingers," the woman said, using the knife to remove the chunk of pumpkin flesh she'd carved.

The piece came free, and Edgar could see at last. His vision cleared bringing the mismatched patterns of a patchwork dress into focus lit by the full moon and flickering candlelight. Her hand touched and lifted his head just as he discovered some of the light was coming from his own eye.

He felt himself being scrutinized for a moment before she spoke. "Ooh, now don't you have a handsome flickerin' soul in there!"

His freshly made jack-o'-lantern eye squinted, failing to bring her face into focus as it released a tear that rolled down a pumpkin groove.

Long arms embraced him and pressed Edgar to a slim bosom. "Oh Hon, don't cry! You're lucky! You just got a new birthday, an' on Halloween too!"

She sat him back straight and angled his head down as he tried to get a look at her. Holding him by the stem, she gave three more thrusts with the knife. "I'll finish up your face and git you inside! I hope you don't mind a birthday party with just me an' Squash-

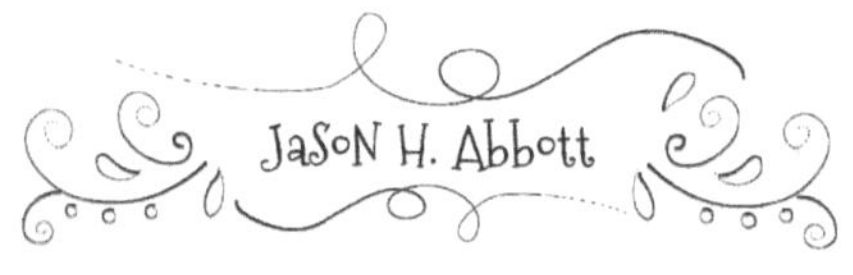

Dog, but I got cakes and cider!"

The blade popped out a new chunk of pumpkin, and Edgar's vision improved gaining another triangle eye. The knife slid right back in again, this time between and under his new eyes.

There were two more stabs as she spoke again. "You don't necessarily *need* a nose, but you'll look funny without one. Trust me."

Edgar scrunched his eyes as the third stroke of the knife left his gourd. He sneezed a moment later, popping out the upside-down triangle she'd carved in him. Catching the chunk of pumpkin, he then rubbed his new hole-nose while she laughed.

Although still mouthless, the flickering soul within him now shone brightly. He studied the triangular peg of pumpkin flesh he held in the illumination his eyes provided, then noticed his hands were slender, green and viny.

Edgar dropped the chunk startled, and quickly grabbed his arms and thighs discovering long, lank limbs otherwise much the same as his fingers. Before

he discovered the rest of the body he now inhabited, he lifted his flickering gaze to the woman helping him.

Her body was lithe, a beanpole frame kneeling in a patchwork dress. She shifted her slim shoulders, leaning in to bring the oval of her pumpkin head level with his own. The square eyes of her jack-o'-lantern face blinked a friendly flutter illumed by the candle-like glow within her.

"Howdy," she said, stretching her already wide pumpkin grin. "I'm Emelia! An' I bet you'd like a mouth to git all your questions out, right?"

Edgar nodded, letting her hand grasp the back of his head.

The knife entered his gourd, and he flinched as Emelia started to saw him another orifice. "Don't squirm, Hon. Mouths are tricky an' I don't wanna git yours crooked. Now, we ain't got no tongues— an' don't ask me how we speak without 'em, 'cause I dunno— but don't worry about me cuttin' yours."

"*Malright,*" he mumbled through the thin slit he

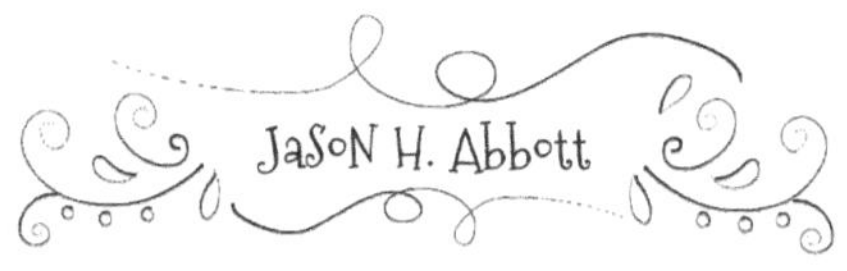

had so far.

"Oh, that's *good!* You're a quick study!"

She turned his head to the side and pulled it lower until it rested on her lap. "What's your name, darlin'?"

His mouth now a little wider, he said his first ungarbled word. "Edgar."

"Oh, that's a nice name. I could git used to sayin' that, *Edgar*."

The sawing of the knife continued in and out, but the pain subsided as quickly as it came. And Emelia worked her craft fast.

"You're turnin' out pretty good," she said, poking out gaps between his teeth. "This is a lot easier than carvin' my own face by myself! The first time I did it just after springin' out of the ground I thought the pumpkin was *on* my head and not my head itself. I bashed holes in it with a rock, an' looked somethin' awful after!"

Her fingers slipping on a handle wet with pump-

kin juice, Emelia pulled out the blade and paused. "The good an' bad of it though is that these old gourds heal up completely in a week. So if you don't take a likin' to what I've done, we can try somethin' else."

She wiped her hand and the handle of the knife dry on the skirt of her dress, then circled her square eyes with a finger. "I'm always redoin' mine just to keep seein' an' talkin'. An' I like playin' with my looks like a hussy! I had round eyes for the longest time!"

Edgar nodded with the half-smile he had so far, then let her turn his head sideways on her lap.

"Almost done," she said as the knife nipped in again.

He waited for Emelia to finish, and his vertically pitched gaze looking to the side found its way to a strange creature watching the both of them. Its thin body resembled a greyhound in shape, but was comprised of twisted vines like Edgar's and what he could see of Emelia's.

However, unlike them, its vines were covered in hairy leaves. A particularly big, droopy pair flopped like ears behind the carved oblong squash it had for a head and snout.

The vegetative canine gave a pant and whine, its own flickering soul-light looking back at him. Seeing Edgar's discomfort in his mistress' lap, it padded a few steps forward. Flinching with squeamishness, Edgar accepted a long lick to the face from a tongue of gooey strings and seeds.

"Awe, he likes you!" Emelia said, pulling out a few pumpkin chunks to finish his mouth. "Squash-Dog's kinda like us, an' kinda not."

She wiped the knife off on her dress again. With her hands removed, Edgar rose from her lap stretching and rubbing a freshly cut mouth.

"The sting will go away real quick," she said sheathing the tool on her belt.

He studied the pumpkin girl as she planted her viny arms to either side of herself. Her glowing smile flickered back at him as she revealed striped tights and buckled shoes sitting cross-legged.

Emelia straightened the bow upon her head stem

with a dainty tug. "Now ain't we just the cutest couple in the pumpkin patch?"

Edgar looked around, finally having a moment to realize that they were, in fact, sitting in a pumpkin patch dappled by shadowy moonlight. The only other illumination come from the soul-flames of the gourd headed trio, and the tin lantern on the ground.

He looked back to her. "We're the *only* couple, Emelia. And a couple of what?"

She shrugged. "Folks an' sages ain't got no names for what we are yet. Most say pumpkin headed weirdo, when I ain't around."

Edgar squinted at her response, then leaned into a stare seeing the old cottage farmhouse not far behind her. "Is that, the witch's house?"

She glanced back. "Yup. Well, used to be, anyways."

He looked down at his viny hands and body. "Used t' be? Where is she? She needs t' change me back!"

"Sorry Hon, they done went an' burned her at the stake 'bout ten years ago."

"Ten years?"

Emelia looked to either side. "Is there an echo in this pumpkin patch? *Yes*. When'd you see her?"

Edgar pinched the brow between the eyes she'd just made for him. "In the third year of the reign of King Phillip the Sixth."

"Alright, I was twenty when I knocked on her door in the *second* year of his reign," she nodded. "He's now been king for nigh *fourteen years*."

His knotty shoulders sagged. "I was twenty-three, and Mother was ailin' when I came knockin'. She had my brother t' still aid her, but..."

Edgar trailed off looking towards the starry curtain obscuring his way back home, then spoke again. "She's probably passed now."

Emelia hugged her knobby knees. "I'm sorry, Hon. Did you come to the hag lookin' for a hex? Somethin' to help your ma?"

He nodded sagging even more, the flicker of his soul-fire downcast and making shadows on the ground. "A spell t' find a good wife. Someone t' help me care for her, and make the farm happy again."

"You sweet man. I came lookin' for a hex to find a husband. Well, a better husband than the one who'd beat an' left me raw, anyways."

Edgar looked back to her, still hunched. "T' bad we couldn't have met on the path t' the witch's house. You didn't deserve no hittin', Emelia. And you're so nice and amiable, I think we'd striked it right off then as now."

"Yesir," Emelia nodded. "I'd bet if we'd found time to talk, we would've shaken on a deal. Given somethin' a go without her hexes an' spells."

"Maybe we wouldn't be in this mess," he sighed.

"Maybe," Emelia said with a wistful, flickered glance. "Maybe we'd just turned around, an' not be talkin' here with pumpkins for heads."

Pulling his own lank knees to a chest of vines, he laid a glum face on folded arms. "Why'd that old hag

do this t' me and you?"

She scooched a little closer. "I'm guessin' that, just like me, that old hag gave you pumpkin seeds that tasted somethin' terrible? But she said to swallow 'em 'cause they were magic an' all?"

Edgar's mouthful of jack-o'-lantern teeth frowned. "They were cursed, weren't they?"

"Nope. Just poisoned!"

He pointed to himself. "And that's why I blacked out? And then she hex-ed me?"

Emelia shook her orange head. "An' that's when you *died*. An' then she buried you in her *garden* with a ritual like she did with me a year prior. We done got our souls turned into *fertilizer*, you and I."

If Edgar's face could pale to match his shocked expression, it would have.

"Oh Sugar, it's alright."

He grabbed his gourd. "I'm so stupid!"

Emelia reached out and touched his hand. "She done got me the same way. You ain't the only pumpkin

head sittin' in the patch, you know."

He looked to her viny green fingers over his. "So, if she killed us, why aren't we in heaven? Or, the other place?"

"You know, I had to walk through two counties after I sprouted up the spring before last to find someone to answer that. An' that ain't easy for a pumpkin head girl!"

Edgar met her warm gaze. "And?"

"Turns out, she wasn't a good witch."

The flame in his empty gourd rolled in hollow eyes. "I know she wasn't a *good* witch, she killed people and turned 'em and their souls into magical fertilizer."

"Not just people. I suspect Squash-Dog would say somethin' similar to us if he said anythin' at all beyond barkin'. An' you ain't even met *Cabbage-Cat* yet, although she's pretty standoffish."

"Well, pets or persons, it isn't a good thing. But why make pumpkin people, squash dogs and, *cabbage cats* outa us?"

Emelia snapped her long fingers. “Oh, I git it! You’re thinkin’ *bad* like she was rotten an’ no good. Which she *was*, but what I mean is that she wasn’t very good at bein’ a witch an’ hexin’.”

Edgar nodded slowly as she spoke, then gradually changed to shaking his head. “And how would you know?”

“Long talk with a good witch two counties over,” she answered. “An’ by that I mean Grazell is good at what she does, in addition to havin’ proper social graces an’ non-murderous proclivities.”

She lifted her arms and gave a sweeping gesture to the pumpkin patch. “Grazell said the old hag done messed an’ muddled her hexin’ up so bad she couldn’t even figure out *what* she was tryin’ to do. That’s probably why nobody remembers her havin’ a bumper crop or anythin’ after stickin’ us in the ground in secret.”

Edgar leaned back and blinked where he sat. “So what does that make us? Mistakes?”

Emelia nodded her gourd as Squash-Dog wandered over and placed his forequarters and head in

her lap. "Grazell thought my soul was, *dislodged* an' trapped in the soil. That eventually it distilled into the little flame now in my noggin an' percolated up to make a new body outta the thing it was supposed to feed."

His jack-o'-lantern face was somber. "And then you took over her cottage and farm?"

"Nobody else wanted it, an' the old hag certainly wasn't usin' the place," she grinned. "I tried movin' back in with Ma an' Pa first, but me bein' a flamin', walkin' plant an' vegetable was *mightily* awkward for all concerned!"

"It must be a strange life," Edgar said, looking at the twisted tendrils that were his hands.

Emelia petted the verdant leaves of Squash-Dog's pelt. "It was pretty lonely before this *melon-mutt* sprouted up last spring. We've kept mostly to ourselves since then, but maybe it'll be a little less lonely if you'd like to hang around?"

"I want t' venture down t' see what's 'come of Mother and Brother at the Farm in the morn'. But t' stroll there with you would be fine, and help with any 'plainin' that I'd need t' do."

"An' then?"

Edgar glanced about the night shrouded farm. "Looks t' me like you could use another pair of arms 'round here."

Squash-Dog jumped off and she rose. Dusting off her dress, Emelia then offered him outstretched hands to help him up. "Sugar, it's a deal."

He stood with a tug from her, a taller beanpole than she was. Standing back, Emelia admired him with a viny hand to her chin.

"Oh, now I do like a tall man!"

"You've got an odd definition of what a 'man' is."

She gave him a poke. "I'll take what I can git. So should you."

Edgar gulped at her flirtation, then looked to the candlelight within the cottage behind them. "You, mentioned cakes and cider?"

"Yes, that's right. Happy Halloween birthday! I

made grandma's sweetcakes to share with me an' the dead, an' now I can share 'em with you, too."

He opened his mouth wide and pointed to the hovering flame within it. "If this is our soul, how do we eat and drink without puttin' it out?"

"Oh, it don't go out," she said, waving away his concern. "I was worried 'bout that for the *longest* time as well. Then Squash-Dog jumped in the river an' kept right on burnin' underwater!"

Emelia reached in and hooked an arm around his before starting to lead him to the house. "Now I go skinny dippin'! If it weren't too cold, I'd take you swimmin' right now as you're already *naked*."

"Naked?!" Edgar shouted, thrusting his free hand down to cover himself. "Stars and garters, I didn't think I had anythin' t' cover!"

She laughed at his antics. "Oh Hon, I don't mind your *dangly root!* I ain't got that, but I do have bumps an' curves an' tucked places under this dress of mine. It ain't like a *regular* woman should be, for sure. But neither are you a regular man."

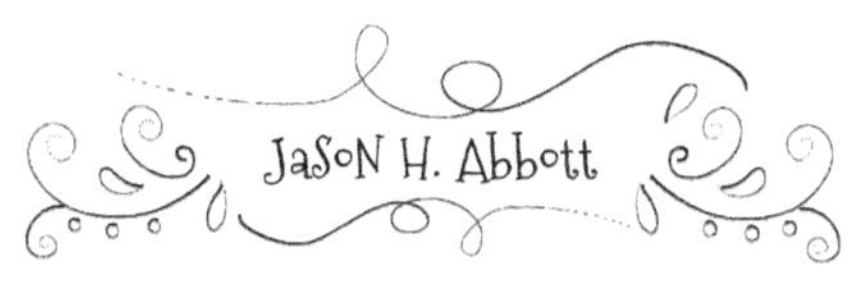

They reached the creaky porch as Edgar spoke. "I admit, I'm intrigued. And perhaps, *oddly unafraid*."

"Then just keep bein' a sweet pumpkin, an' I'll likely show you a snuggly patch to plant yourself in," Emelia said with a puff of flame. "In the mornin' we'll strip the scarecrow an' git you somethin' to wear."

Squash-Dog clattered up the steps and past their ankles. With the gourd-headed canine pawing the door as they reached it, Edgar paused.

"Maybe we'll get what we wanted, after all?" he asked.

They opened the door together, and Emelia's smile literally lit the room. "Welcome home!"

Jason H. Abbott is an author of fantasy, science fiction and more. Born a lobsterman's son in a small coastal town, he spent his youth exploring the woods and rocky beaches of Maine pursuing make-believe and adventures. These journeys eventually led him down many paths less traveled, and to a storyteller's life where the power of myths both ancient and modern are his inspirations.

An active indie and social media author, Jason shares daily original micro and flash fiction between working on longer projects. These include several ongoing microfiction series and miniseries', and numerous one-shot "very short stories" often no longer than a Twitter tweet. You can learn more about Jason, his available works, and follow him across many platforms by visiting his author's site at JasonHAbbott.com.

www.ingramcontent.com/pod-product-compliance
Lightning Source LLC
Chambersburg PA
CBHW022045050726
47591CB00003B/960

* 9 7 8 1 9 5 1 4 7 8 0 2 5 *